The Race
Doobesh

A Magical World Awaits You
Read

THE SECRETS OF DROON

The Race to Doobesh

by Tony Abbott
Illustrated by David Merrell
Cover illustration by Tim Jessell

A
LITTLE APPLE
PAPERBACK

SCHOLASTIC INC.
New York Toronto London Auckland Sydney
Mexico City New Delhi Hong Kong Buenos Aires

To my mother
with love always

For more information about the continuing saga of Droon,
please visit Tony Abbott's website at
www.tonyabbottbooks.com

ISBN-13: 978-0-439-66158-4
ISBN-10: 0-439-66158-7

18 17 16 15 14 13 12 11 10 9 8 7   8 9 10 11 12/0

Printed in the U.S.A.
First printing, January 2005

Contents

One

Eyes of the Spy

"That was incredibly awesome!"

"Awesomely incredible!"

"Plus, extremely cool."

Eric Hinkle and his friends Julie Rubin and Neal Kroger stumbled a little as they made their way out of the dark and into the bright, sunlit lobby of the movie theater.

"The most amazing part," said Neal, squinting at the light, then slipping on a pair of sunglasses, "was that elf guy with the dark spectacles and the funny name —"

"Sneaky!" said Julie. "I loved his green boots."

Neal grinned. "I loved when he put on his elf glasses and did all that incredible action stuff. I could do that —"

"The wizard was very cool, too," said Eric. "It was amazing the way his magic freed the trolls."

The lobby was full of people, some lining up for the next showing of the movie, others still straggling out of the dark theater.

Julie sighed. "Remember when the princess said that every adventure is a journey and every journey is an adventure? How fabulous was that?"

Eric couldn't help but smile. The movie they had just seen *was* fabulous. It was full of adventure and action and magical special effects.

But it wasn't as fabulous as their real lives.

Their real lives in Droon, that is.

Droon was a world of wizards and sorcerers, of strange creatures, gleaming cities, misty islands, and endless seas. It was a realm of magic and adventure the three friends had discovered one day beneath Eric's basement. Since then, they had gone to Droon many times, descending an enchanted staircase that connected the two worlds.

On their very first journey to Droon, they had met Keeah, a real princess who turned out to be a wizard just learning her powers. She had become their best Droon friend. Together with Keeah, an old wizard named Galen, who was now on a long journey, and a friendly spider troll named Max, Eric and his friends had helped Droon battle its enemies many times. Eric and Julie had even gained magical powers. Julie could fly, and Eric was turning into a full-fledged wizard himself.

As he looked around the lobby, Eric saw some other classmates from school. He waved to them. He knew that if he ever told any of them about Droon, it would sound made up. It would sound like a movie.

But he, Neal, and Julie wouldn't tell anyone. Long ago, Galen had told them that Droon was a secret they had to protect. If anyone in the Upper World ever found out about it, there was no telling what strange things might happen.

"Okay, guys," said Julie, checking her watch. "My mom expects us in five minutes. We'll have supper at my house."

"Supper in five minutes?" said Neal. "Perfect. That leaves just enough time."

"Time for what?" asked Julie.

"To get a snack, of course," said Neal.

Eric chuckled. "Neal, you're supposed to get popcorn going *into* the movie, not when you come *out*."

Neal shrugged and trotted off to the food counter. "Call me a rebel. . . ."

Shaking their heads, Eric and Julie followed their friend and waited while he stood in line.

"Eric," whispered Julie, "did the sorcerer in the movie remind you of anyone?"

"Of course," he said in a low voice. "Lord Sparr. Before."

Right. Lord Sparr. *Before.*

Sparr was a sorcerer. Always dressed in black, he had real purple fins growing behind his ears. As long as the children had known Sparr, he had been trying to take over all of Droon for himself.

Until now.

Not long ago, on the creepy Isle of

Mists, Sparr had used a spell to wake up Emperor Ko from his charmed sleep. Ko had been the terrible leader of the dark and frightening beasts of Goll. He had kidnapped Sparr from the Upper World when Sparr was only an infant and brought him up in Droon's Dark Lands. For years, Sparr's goal had been to wake the sleeping emperor. Together, the two powerful sorcerers would be impossible to beat.

But when Sparr woke up Emperor Ko and brought him into modern Droon, something unbelievable had happened. In the middle of the spell, Sparr himself had been zapped back into a boy.

Lord Sparr was now . . . Kid Sparr!

And after being Droon's enemy for ages, Sparr was now helping Keeah to stop Emperor Ko's plans. On their first adventure together, Kid Sparr had even saved Eric's life!

Eric still couldn't believe it. "With Sparr

on our side now," he whispered, "things in Droon sure are strange."

"Uh, they're a little strange here, too," said Julie, making a face. "Is Neal really talking to his food?"

Eric turned to see his friend staring down into a jumbo container of popcorn.

"Could you say that again, please?" asked Neal.

Julie and Eric quickly pulled Neal to a corner of the crowded lobby. There, they bent their heads to the popcorn, too. As they listened, they heard a faint but very clear voice whispering from the buttery kernels. It was saying the same thing over and over.

Find . . . the . . . dragon!

Neal peered around the lobby through his dark glasses. "I don't think there are any dragons here."

"Not here," said Eric. "That voice is from Droon. It must be."

He glanced through the lobby doors to the late afternoon sky outside. Barely visible over the library across the street was the outline of a nearly full, silver moon.

He said what they were all thinking.

"Could the voice be talking about the moon dragon?" he whispered. "You know, Gethwing?"

They all knew about Gethwing.

Eric, Neal, and Julie had crossed paths with the creature once already. Strange and terrifying, Gethwing was a four-winged, powerful dragon and the right-hand beast of Emperor Ko. He had taken care of young Sparr when the boy was growing up in Ko's palace.

Find . . . the . . . dragon! the voice repeated.

Eric felt himself tense up. Suddenly, the hair on the back of his neck tickled. His heart began to pound. As he carefully scanned the crowds lining up for the next movie, he said, "It feels like someone —"

"Is watching us?" said Julie, lowering her voice. She, too, glanced around.

"A spy?" said Neal. "There was a spy in the movie. That fishy-looking creature."

"I felt it yesterday, too," said Eric. "I've been wondering whether somebody in the big house on my street heard us talking about . . . you-know-where."

"Somebody might think it's weird that we're listening to popcorn, too," said Julie. "Either way, we have to go to you-know-where right now. If someone is watching us, we need to throw them off our trail. We need to be sneaky —"

"Sneaky?" Neal grinned. "I love when you call me that!"

Finishing his popcorn and tossing the box into a container by the doors, Neal darted out of the lobby to Main Street. He crouched low, glanced both ways, then scampered behind the nearest mailbox, leaped over a bench, and dashed into the park. "Forward, elves!" he called back.

Laughing, Julie and Eric ran after him.

Zipping past the library, they headed down a side street, sprinted in front of the pizza place, and dodged behind the supermarket into a neighborhood of houses.

Weaving across front yards and along driveways, they were out of breath when they finally reached Eric's back door.

"There was probably an easier way to get here," said Julie. "But I guess adventure heroes never take the easy way!"

As they tumbled through Eric's back door and into the kitchen, Julie and Neal peeked out the window into the backyard.

"No one," said Julie. "I think we lost him."

Neal nodded, then grumbled. "I think I lost my sunglasses, too."

"We'll hunt for them later," said Eric. "For now, let's go find a dragon!"

The three friends tramped down the basement stairs. Nearly hidden under the staircase was a small door blocked by large cartons. The kids quickly pushed the cartons aside, opened the door, and piled into a tiny closet.

"Ready to find a dragon?" asked Eric.

"Ready," said Julie.

Neal nodded. "I guess I'd rather find a dragon than have a dragon find us!"

Eric closed the door and gave a tug on the string of the ceiling light. It clicked off, and the little room was dark for a second. Then it wasn't.

Whooosh! The floor became the top step of a glittering staircase, curving away from the house. Descending through the clouds, the kids entered a bright, warm afternoon. The sun shone over a wide blue sea and on the fluffy bushes and squat green buildings of a small village clinging to the top of a mountain. The village was surrounded by a wall.

"Firefrog Mountain!" said Neal. "We've been here before."

Firefrog Mountain was the home of the green-flamed animals known as firefrogs. They watched over creatures and people who had made trouble in Droon.

The kids leaped off the steps and onto a narrow path snaking up the mountainside toward the village at the top. At the same moment, a creature came barreling down the path toward them.

"Hurry! Hurry!" it cried.

"Oh, my gosh!" said Julie. "A . . . a . . . *dragon*!"

It was a dragon, all right. But as it came

closer, the friends could see that it wasn't the frightening moon dragon they had feared. This dragon was plump and squat, with spiky brown skin, a thick tail, and two small wings. It was wearing an apron covered in fruit stains and there was a puffy chef's hat on its knobby head.

"It's Jabbo!" said Eric. "The pie maker!"

"Jabbo, stop!" called Neal.

A humble pie maker in the Upper World, Jabbo had once come upon an ancient spell and used it to try to take over Droon. After the kids had helped stop him, Galen had sent him here, to Firefrog Mountain.

When the little dragon saw the children now, he screamed, turned, and hustled right back to the village. "No more pie!" he growled. "No more *anything*! Jabbo is done! Jabbo is escaping! Good-bye!"

Two

On (and Off) Firefrog Mountain

Flapping his small wings as fast as he could, and jumping with all his strength, Jabbo bounced over the village wall and disappeared.

"Come on!" said Eric. Together the three friends scrambled up the path and helped one another over the wall. "After him!"

"After him?" chirped a voice. "We're *already* after him!"

Fwish! An eight-legged spider troll swung down from the wall on a string of silky thread and plopped into the street next to the children.

"Max!" said Julie.

"And Keeah, too!" said Max, his orange hair standing on end.

Just then, Keeah rushed into the street, her blond hair flying. She was followed by a dozen squealing frogs, their skin blazing with cool green flames.

"I'm glad you came," she said to the children as they joined in the chase. "Jabbo escaped from his little house this morning. He claimed his kitchen was haunted —"

"Haunted," repeated Max. "By a ghostly voice."

Julie blinked. "We heard a voice! It told us to 'find the dragon' —"

"Finding him is not catching him!" came a shout. "Everyone, this way!"

A figure in a long black cloak dropped down from a nearby rooftop into an open square. It was a boy about their age, with fins growing behind his ears.

It was Sparr.

"Follow me, if you want to catch Jabbo." He dashed across the square to the far side. Everyone followed him into a narrow passage between two buildings. Running ahead to the next corner, he slowed and then stopped, holding up his hand to the others, and said, "Careful . . ."

As they listened for sounds, Sparr turned slightly. "Eric, I'm glad you're back."

"Hey, me, too," Eric whispered. "And listen . . . thanks again for saving me last time. I'm really sorry I didn't trust you at first."

Sparr smiled. "When I think about who I became, I wouldn't trust me, either."

Eric glanced back at his friends. It was still hard to think of their greatest enemy helping them. But he felt that Sparr really was trying to be different. He knew that with the boy on their side, at least, they might actually make a difference in Droon.

Sparr on their side. It felt good.

Weird, but good.

"Watch out!" cried a firefrog. "Heads up!"

Suddenly — *whooooosh! whooooosh! whooooosh!* — the air was full of flying pie plates. One spun past Neal's ear and nearly struck Julie. Another slammed against the wall behind them and clattered to the cobblestones in the square, while a third flew at the firefrogs, scattering them.

"Jabbo will never be caught!" the pie maker yelled, leaning down from a balcony overhead. In a flash, he scrambled from roof to roof all the way to the far side of the square, dropped onto an awning,

then bounced up and over the village wall again.

"He's outside again!" said Keeah. "Eric, Sparr, with me. Max, Neal, the wall. Julie —"

"I'll fly!" she said. With a quick flutter of her arms, Julie launched herself over the buildings to a narrow ledge just outside the village wall. When Eric, Keeah, and Sparr came bounding over the high wall, they found her hovering above the ledge just as Jabbo came hustling down.

Julie crossed her arms. "Stop right there, mister!"

"Ohh!" growled the chubby little dragon. He spun around on his knobby heels, but Keeah was blocking the way. Neal and Max, together with the firefrogs, were crowded along the wall looking down at him.

"We have you now, Jabbo," said Keeah. "Time to go back to your little house before you hurt yourself —"

"Never!" the little dragon said, wobbling on the ledge. His eyes were full of fear. "Jabbo won't go back until *he* goes away. The ghostly voice! It's haunting poor Jabbo!"

Eric frowned. "Whose voice is it?"

"Someone who likes to whisper over and over," the little dragon grumbled. "And over and over he says the same thing. *'Find the gate . . . find the gate.'* Find the gate?! This is Firefrog Mountain. There aren't any gates —"

Suddenly — *squawkkkk!* — the clouds above them tore open, and two giant winged creatures swooped down. Covered with ragged gray feathers, they had long beaks, clawed arms, and burning red eyes.

"Beasts!" hissed Sparr. "I know those two. They work for Ko —"

Before anyone could stop them, the beasts dived for Jabbo, clutched him between them, and shot back into the sky, cawing and shrieking.

"Help me!" Jabbo called back. "Never mind voices — let Jabbo bake pies again!"

But the beasts disappeared into the clouds with him. In a flash, they were gone.

The firefrogs gasped.

The children stared up at the sky.

"We found the dragon," said Julie. "Then we lost him . . . to the beasts!"

"Why did the beasts take Jabbo?" asked Neal. "Do they have a thing for pies?"

Sparr shook his head. "No. I know I don't remember everything about my life with Ko, but beast language is one thing I'll never forget. Those two are taking Jabbo far away. They're taking him to Doobesh."

Max shivered. "Doobesh? The Ruby Orb of Doobesh stole me away once!"

The kids had never been to Doobesh, but they had all heard of it. It was a strange city of towers and turrets in the southernmost part of Droon, on the edge of Ko's Dark Lands.

"But why are they taking Jabbo there?" asked Eric, still searching the sky.

Everyone turned to Sparr. Rubbing his forehead, he sighed, then spoke.

"Doobesh is one of the five Magic Cities in Droon," he said. "For ages, it's been the center of stealing and trading in magic, a gathering place of thieves and pirates. And now — I guess — of beasts, too. But why they are taking Jabbo there, I don't know."

Julie frowned. "Well, the voice told us to find the dragon. Then it told Jabbo to find the gate. Maybe this is like a treasure hunt. If Jabbo is going to Doobesh, maybe the gate is there, too."

"And maybe the voice is, too," added Neal.

Keeah gazed at the empty sky. "Then let's find out. I say we go to Doobesh, and we go the fastest way I know. Everyone ready? Hang on —"

With a swift motion, the princess twirled her hands high, and a bright blue wind spun instantly around the six friends, lifting them into the open air. Waving to the firefrogs, they flew up and away over the Sea of Droon.

To the Magic City of Doobesh.

Three

Follow the . . . What?

The blue light sparkled like glitter stirred quickly in a glass of water.

As the children spun faster and faster, the lakes, rivers, and deserts of Droon passed beneath them and vanished into the distance.

"Hold tight!" said Neal. "It's a long way down there."

"I won't let go," said Max. "Don't *you* let go!"

When, finally, the spinning slowed, a city of golden turrets, purple towers, green roofs, and high orange walls came into view.

"There it is," said Sparr. "Doobesh."

The city was perched in the middle of sandy plains surrounded by clusters of big-leafed palm trees. As the kids descended through the air, they saw many streets of low, crooked buildings. Arching over the streets were bridges covered by flowering vines. In a large central square, before a building that looked like a palace, stood a fountain bubbling brightly with crystal-clear water.

Julie breathed in. "For a dangerous magical city, Doobesh sure is beautiful."

"Yeah," said Neal. "Not the usual beast hangout."

"Just so," chirped Max. "I see no Doobeshians. They are short, furry creatures always dressed in long, green capes. But the city looks deserted. What's going on?"

"Let's keep to the shadows and try to find out," said Keeah. Leaning first one way, then the other, she set them down gently in a narrow alley between two low shops. As soon as the blue light flickered out, they slipped under the shadow of a striped awning.

A moment later, a wisp of blue-tinted fog rolled down the street toward them.

Keeah gasped. "Oh, no —"

"What?" said Sparr. "What is it?"

"Fog pirates!" whispered Keeah. "They plunder the towns of southern Droon."

"Fog pirates?" said Julie. "What are they doing here —"

"What are *we* doing here?" growled a deep voice suddenly. "What are *you* doing here?" An instant later, the fog dissolved and there stood a stout, bear-faced man. He was dressed in a ragged coat, with a red bandanna around his head and a black patch over one eye. Wisps of fog clung to his tall black boots.

Behind him stood several other mean-faced pirates as well as some furry, green-caped Doobeshians. They carried a big black net that Eric feared was not meant for catching fish.

"Fog pirates!" said Sparr, his eyes wide.

"*Captain* of the fog pirates!" snapped the patch-eyed man. He looked down on the kids with a broken-toothed grin. "Princess Keeah! You might remember me. I'm Yoho. I fought you and Galen more than once, I think!"

"More than twice, I think!" Max grumbled.

The pirate laughed. "And we'd be

crossing swords now if we didn't have bigger problems. Here, take a look that way!"

The kids turned around and glanced down the alley into a small square beyond.

Even as they looked, they saw the square fill up with creatures of all shapes and sizes. They slithered in from the side streets or dropped suddenly from the sky. They came in ones and twos. Some had great dark wings, others had hooves. Some were covered with ragged fur, while still others bore spikes, scales, and fins.

Eric felt his heart beat faster. All the creatures, no matter how strange, had one thing in common. Each had deep red eyes, burning in their heads like fiery coals. It was their burning red eyes that marked them as beasts — servants of Emperor Ko.

"Beasts!" Keeah gasped. "Dozens of them. Hundreds!"

"They've been gathering for weeks," said Yoho.

"But why?" asked Sparr. "Why are Ko's beasts here? And why now?"

The pirate grunted. "Because of the dragon!"

"The dragon!" repeated the Doobeshians.

Eric blinked. "You mean Jabbo the pie maker? He's already here —"

"I mean Gethwing the moon dragon!" grunted Yoho. "He flew in a little while ago. All the beasts that have come are going to the palace to see him. Doobesh, my young friends, has been taken over!"

"Taken over!" said the Doobeshians. "And we don't like it!"

Keeah turned to her friends. "If Jabbo was brought here to Gethwing, we'd better get to the palace and rescue Jabbo before . . . well, just before."

"And who will rescue us?" asked Yoho, blinking as he shifted his patch from one eye to the other. "We're pirates, sure, but times have changed. Back in the good old days — well, last month — we ruled the seas. The sea witch Demither used to help us attack ships for treasure. But even she's gone now."

"Gone?" asked Sparr. "Where did Demither go?"

Yoho shrugged. "This is what I'm saying! The beasts must have scared her away!"

"Not only that," said one of the green-caped creatures. "But the beasts have stolen all the magic from Doobesh!"

"They've even stolen the *stolen* magic!" growled Yoho. "Those red-eyed monsters found our secret treasure hideout and stole everything! I ask you — what's happening to good old Droon?"

"Good old Droon!" echoed the Doobeshians together.

It was strange to hear the fog pirates talk like that, Eric thought, but he found that he himself felt the same way. Since the beasts had come back to Droon, things were getting stranger and stranger. For one thing, he would never have believed he and his friends would be chatting with the dreaded fog pirates!

Suddenly, the beasts gathering in the square gave out a great howl. "To the palace! To see Gethwing!"

At once, they all began to crawl, slither, and stomp out of the square, heading away from the group in the alley.

"We have to go to the palace, too," said Eric. "We still have to find the dragon. Whether that means Gethwing or Jabbo, I guess we'll find out."

"Wait until the beasties leave," said

Yoho. "Then, if you really want to find the palace, all you have to do is follow the slime. But be careful. With those beasts here, and no magic, things are different in Droon now!"

As the children stared at the last of the beasts, a thin fog swept around Yoho and his mates again, and the little group drifted to the corner and vanished.

Max began to mutter. "Follow the *slime*? Well, I suppose we'd best be going —"

"Good idea, Max," said Keeah. "We'll follow your lead."

"Perfect," added Sparr. "Thanks, Max."

The spider troll blinked. "Well, you don't *all* have to agree! But never mind. Follow me, then. And let's all try to stay in the shadows!"

With Max in front, the kids moved slowly and carefully to the end of the alley and entered the square. The beasts were gone, but several blobs of slime led from the square and into a narrow street on the far side.

"These beasts should really wash their feet," whispered Neal. "If they even *have* feet!"

Max led the children into one twisting alley after another, moving from one slimy footprint to the next. Although the sun was shining brightly in the streets, they kept to the shadows cast by the bridges overhead.

"I still don't know why the beasts would want Jabbo," said Eric.

"Galen always said that everything has a reason," said Keeah. "The tough part is figuring out what it is."

Neal chuckled. "That sounds like me and math."

Max stopped at the end of a narrow side street, and the children peered carefully ahead. Before them stood the main city square. Crowded on every side of the square were the dark beasts they had seen earlier, their red eyes blazing. They stood there nearly motionless, as if they were waiting for something to happen.

All at once, a roar exploded from the beasts. "Gethwing! Gethwing!"

As one, the beasts bowed, lowering their heads to the ground.

At the same moment — *sssst!* — a great, loud hissing noise came from a street across the square. It was followed almost immediately by the appearance of two huge snakes, slithering from the street and into the square.

"Come on, quickly!" hissed Sparr, looking up. "To the rooftop. We need to get a better view of Gethwing —"

"This way!" said Keeah. She jumped onto a barrel in the side street, grabbed a vine dangling from above, and hoisted her-self to the corner roof. Sparr went next, then Neal, Eric, Julie, and Max. Looking carefully over the crowd of beasts, they watched the snakes drag a large golden cart into the square.

Inside the cart was a throne encrusted with jewels. And on the throne sat a dragon wearing a crown and robe of gleaming gold and blue.

When the cart drew closer, the kids fi-nally saw the dragon's face.

It was covered with purple pie filling.

"That's not a moon dragon," whispered Eric. "It's a *pie* dragon. It's . . . Jabbo!"

Four

Some Kind of Dragon

It *was* Jabbo. He stood up from his throne and glowered at the beasts.

"Steady on, my snaky fellows!" cried the pie maker. "Left, then right. And not too bumpy now!"

"Yes-s-s, Gethwing-g-g-g!" the snakes said.

The beasts on every side of the square kept chanting "Gethwing!" and bowing as Jabbo's cart rolled past.

"What — what — I mean — *what is going on here*?" sputtered Julie.

Glancing over the heads of the bowing beasts, Jabbo suddenly spied the children on the rooftop. His eyes widened. He flinched.

"He looks afraid," said Keeah.

"And maybe glad to see us," said Eric.

Keeping his eyes fixed on the kids, and careful not to let the beasts see, Jabbo pointed into his hand and nodded toward where a bridge arched over the square ahead. It was thick with hanging flowers.

"I think he wants us to go to him!" whispered Sparr.

While the beasts still chanted — "Gethwing!" — the friends darted across the rooftops until they reached the bridge. When the snakes dragged Jabbo's cart underneath, the kids dropped into it one by one.

"Oh!" Jabbo whispered, when they were all huddled inside the cart with him. "Jabbo is so glad to see you!"

"What have you gotten yourself mixed up in?" asked Keeah. "These are real beasts, you know. Are you playing some kind of trick?"

"No!" whispered the little dragon. "These beasts — guess what? — think that *Jabbo* is Gethwing!" He raised his voice and called to the snakes, "Go right!"

Thwunk! The snakes slammed into a wall.

"No, the *other* right!" snapped Jabbo. The beasts backed up and slithered the other way.

Sparr laughed quietly. "They think *you* are Gethwing? You don't really fit the part!"

"True!" said Jabbo. "Here's what happened. The beasts were told by Ko to find Gethwing for a special mission. Okay, but after four hundred years of sleeping, all they remembered was that Gethwing was some kind of dragon. *Some kind of dragon!* When those two brutes saw Jabbo on Fire-frog Mountain, they thought they had their dragon. So Jabbo has had to pretend to be that big bad dragon the whole time!"

"Gethwing has a special mission?" said Sparr. "What special mission?"

Jabbo made a grunting sound. "Oh, yes. About that. The reason the beasts have taken over Doobesh, the reason Gethwing is supposed to be here, is because Doobesh is the only place — wait, Jabbo will show you. Snakes, to the palace! Gethwing needs to rest!"

While the beasts still bowed and cheered, the snakes circled the square and stopped in front of the large palace.

"Now, beasts," said Jabbo, "how about one more big bow?"

"GETH-WINGGGG!" the beasts wailed. When every beast's head was bent low, Jabbo urged the children swiftly from the cart into the palace.

Once safely inside, the pie maker hustled the children quickly to a terrace overlooking the plains east of Doobesh. The plains spread out toward smoke-covered lands in the distance. Eric knew they were Emperor Ko's Dark Lands.

"Remember the voice that said to find the gate?" said the pie maker. "Guess what? The voice is quiet now. Because Jabbo found the gate." He pointed toward the distant sands. "There it is."

Keeah looked out over the plains, scanning the entire scene from right to left and back again. "I don't see a gate. What are we looking at?"

"What? Oh, Jabbo forgot," said the little dragon. "Because he is a dragon, Jabbo can see what the beasts can see. And what normal people can't see —"

Sparr breathed out a long sigh. "I can see it."

"You can?" said Eric.

Sparr waved his hand in front of their faces. Suddenly, far across the plains, on the border of the Dark Lands, they saw a giant wooden gate rising up behind a cluster of trees.

"Holy cow, the gate!" asked Julie. "Where does it lead?"

"To Bleakwold," said Sparr suddenly. His face turned pale even as he said the word. "It's deep in the Dark Lands."

Max grumbled. "Bleakwold? I don't like the sound of that. As a matter of fact, I don't like the sound of any of this."

"*You* don't like it?" snorted Jabbo. "As Gethwing the Totally Fearsome, Jabbo is actually supposed to lead the beasts to the gate! Then they'll all cross Bleakwold to journey to a thing called the magic forge."

Eric kept looking at Sparr. "The magic forge? A forge for what?"

"Ko's magic battle armor," said Sparr. "Not just his armor, either, but all the beast armor is forged there, using magical objects and devices. Wearing it, the beasts become invincible. And they'll wear it to attack Jaffa City."

"Attack Jaffa City? Attack Jaffa City!" cried Max. "Ko is . . . is . . . *evil*!"

Keeah breathed deeply. "We've gotten this far by following clues. But I think we can figure out the next step all by ourselves. We have to destroy that forge."

"From what the beasts say, it will be hazardous," said Jabbo. "Tricky, too. Plus also quite dangerous."

Max grunted. "Yes, well, tell us something we don't know —"

"How about extremely deadly?" said Sparr. He was rubbing his forehead as if he were remembering something. "To protect his forge, Ko filled Bleakwold with obstacles deadly to everyone but beasts. I remember that well enough."

The kids stood looking out at the Dark Lands until Sparr's visibility charm ended and they could no longer see the gate.

Jabbo sighed. "The beasts won't go to the forge until Jabbo gives the order. Maybe you can get there before they do. Jabbo can try to stall the beasts as long as possible. Well, he can try to try —"

"Thank you, Jabbo," said Keeah. "I know you're afraid."

The pie maker made a tiny noise. "Afraid? Do you hear that chattering sound? That is Jabbo's teeth! But what's right is right. And beasts all over Droon is not right."

"Good," said Sparr. "For us, the safest way — the *only* way — into Bleakwold is by challenging the beasts at their own game. We'll become beasts. . . ."

Neal blinked. "Excuse me? *Become* beasts? I don't like red eyes."

Sparr half smiled. "I seem to remember a spell that will change us into beasts for a little while."

"You *seem* to remember a spell?" said Keeah. "How well do you *seem* to remember it?"

"Pretty well," he said.

"This doesn't sound so good to me," said Julie. "There must be another way. Anyone have another idea? Anyone? Anything? Please?"

The beasts roared outside the palace, and the kids stared silently at one another.

"I guess it's settled," said Sparr. "I need to put you — put us — into a deep sleep.

The spell will take until morning to work. Trust me."

"Jabbo can hide you until morning, and come back for you just before dawn," said the dragon. Then he led them quickly into a long yellow room filled with puffy beds. "Oh, Jabbo does hope this works!"

"*You* hope it works?" muttered Eric, climbing into a bed between Neal and Max.

As Sparr closed his eyes and began to mumble strange words, Eric thought of a time in the sorcerer's volcano palace so long ago. He and Keeah had been holding their breath, hiding from a terrifying monster, when it transformed right before their eyes, from a hideous beast into the grown-up Sparr. Only a pair of fins was left as a reminder.

"Just close your eyes," said Sparr.

Eric already felt sleepy. "Oh . . . man . . ."

The last thing he saw was Julie's nose. It was beginning to grow.

Too tired to watch, Eric closed his eyes.

First one, then another. Then another . . . and another.

Five

A Tour of Bleakwold

The sound of beasts roaring and shrieking woke Eric. Opening his eyes, he looked at himself in the early morning light. He was taller and wider than usual. He was also covered with fur the color and length of mown grass.

When he climbed out of bed, he found he kept slumping over onto all fours. And when he blinked, he remembered closing his eyes the night before. All four of them.

Two eyes were in the front of his head, two peered out the back.

He could tell from the glow around him that they burned with a bright red light.

"Hey, Julie, Neal," he said, even though they were on different sides of the room.

Julie was her normal height, but quite round. From the tip of her long, flat snout to the ends of her thick, three-toed feet, she was covered with patchy blue fur. Claws stuck out from the ends of her short arms.

Neal was much smaller than the others and looked as if he were wearing a suit of armor made up of tiny scales. "I'M A FISH!" he shouted loudly. "HEY, I'M A FISH AND I SHOUT! PLUS, I HAVE THREE FEET! AND THEY STINK —"

"Neal, shh!" hissed Sparr. Towering over the fishy Neal, he looked like an upright wolf, but with ears the size of dinner plates. "Quiet, please," he whispered. "You're a beast called a Loudertail —"

"TAIL? I HAVE A TAIL!" Neal shouted, trying to look behind himself.

Julie laughed when she saw Neal. "Glup-glup-glup!" She stopped. "Glup?"

"Uh, yeah, sorry, Julie," whispered Sparr. "You're a beast called a Glup. I think that's all you can say."

Achoo! Julie sneezed suddenly, and a blast of icy air shot into the room.

"Well, and sneeze ice, too," said Sparr.

Next to Julie, Keeah was all wings and feathers, but curling up from her forehead she had a pair of long, twisted antlers. "These will be trouble, I just know it," she said.

Finally, Max loped over to them. He was shaped something like a cat, covered with sleek orange fur, but with bony spikes running down his back. "Only four paws?" he asked. "How will I manage?"

As different as his friends now were, Eric saw that the same smoldering red light burned in all of their eyes. They were all beasts, with the same eyes every beast had.

"Just as long as you know how to end the spell, Sparr," said Eric. "Wait, you *do* know how to end it, don't you?"

Before Sparr could answer, Jabbo hurried in, flapping his wings rapidly. Then he stopped, his eyes wide. "Oh, dear! You are . . . well, never mind. The beasts are ready to go, so you must sneak out before them. A secret passage the pirates built will take you outside the walls. And please hurry. Jabbo fears how long he can delay the beasts!"

"Or how long before the real Gethwing arrives," added Sparr.

The dragon's jaw dropped. "Now Jabbo is very afraid. Go, before it's too late!"

As quickly as they could, the kids waddled, stomped, and slithered through the halls of the palace and down into a narrow passage through the city walls.

When they finally slipped out onto the plains outside Doobesh, each of the kids could see the giant wooden gate to Bleakwold in the distance. Turning one last time, they saw Jabbo standing on the palace terrace, his back to them. Just inside the city gate, they knew, were the beasts, anxious to begin their journey to Bleakwold.

"Ahem!" shouted Jabbo, clearing his throat and flapping his wings. "As the great and all-powerful b-b-beast known as G-G-G —"

The beasts all over the city roared, "Gethwing!"

"—I will send you to the Bleakwold gate!"

"Gethwing!" they shouted again.

"But before G-G-Gethwing gives you all the command to go," Jabbo added quickly, "you must hear about a night long, long ago. Well, it wasn't a night, actually, it was more like late afternoon. Jabbo was flapping his wings — and when I say Jabbo, I mean Gethwing, who is me. And when I say I was flapping my wings, I really mean a friend and I were flapping our wings. My wings, his wings, several wings . . . which rhymes with sings and reminds me of another story. . . ."

"CAN'T LISTEN," shouted Neal. "TOO PAINFUL."

"I hope Jabbo has lots of stories," said Sparr.

Keeah shook her antlers. "Come on, beasties."

As quickly and carefully as they could, the children and Max sneaked away from the Doobesh walls and across the plains toward the great wooden gate of Bleak-wold.

Every minute, the sky above them grew smokier. The sun that shone over Doobesh was nearly hidden by thick air drifting in from the Dark Lands.

"This is what happens when beasts go somewhere," said Sparr. "Everything turns dark, smoky, and hopeless."

"Let's hope it's temporary," said Eric.

"Glup!" added Julie.

After nearly an hour of quick traveling, the band of beasts arrived at the Bleakwold gate.

It was far larger than it had looked from Doobesh. It stretched very wide and very high into the smoky sky. As Keeah walked up to it, Sparr stopped suddenly in the shadow of the gate. "Wait. I hear it! That voice again. I hear it —"

"WHAT?" shouted Neal. "IS THERE MORE STUFF TO FIND?"

Sparr shut his eyes tight and cupped his hands behind his huge ears, listening. "The voice is coming from inside the gate. It's saying, '*Find . . . the . . . cave —*' "

All of a sudden, Eric discovered that the eyes in the back of his head were extremely strong. He squinted back across the distance and saw the gates of Doobesh opening and the army of beasts charging out. "Jabbo must have run out of stories, because the beasts are on their way."

"We need to get into Bleakwold now," said Keeah. She sent a powerful blast of violet sparks at the wooden gate, but it fizzled and vanished into nothing. "Uh . . ."

"The Dark Lands," said Sparr. "Wizard powers don't work here."

"BUT MAYBE JUST BEING A BEAST WILL WORK!" shouted Neal. "GATES — OPPPENNNN!"

Neal roared so loudly that the ground shuddered and shook, quivered and quaked, until finally — *errrrr!* — the Bleak-wold gate creaked open before them.

"Oh, dear me!" said Max.

"Glup!" added Julie.

Even as he stared ahead through the open gate, Eric kept two eyes on Doobesh. And there, just above the dust pluming up over the charging beasts, he spied the pale silvery moon. It was now full and reminded him of the moon he had noticed at home. Remembering the movie he and his friends had seen that afternoon, Eric smiled. They were on a real adventure now.

"Come on, beasties," said Keeah. "We haven't got much time."

As soon as everyone marched through

the gate, they knew right away they were in a different kind of place. The entire sky was covered with dark low clouds. Smoke and fog drifted everywhere. And the air was hot and steamy. But that wasn't all.

"Oh!" said Max, standing on two feet. "Someone mentioned *obstacles*?"

A river of flames wove this way and that across the charred black earth. It started from far in the distance and wove all the way across the plain ahead of them. Flames leaped and curled twenty feet high as far as they could see.

"WE HAVE TO CROSS THAT?" Neal yelled. "WHY DID KO MAKE THIS SO HARD? I'M PRETTY SURE YELLING WILL NOT GET US THROUGH THAT!"

Sparr stared at the flaming river. "Beasts travel in groups. If one doesn't have the powers, another will —"

All at once, Julie jumped. "Glup!"

"WHAT IS IT?" shouted Neal.

"Glu-uu-uu-up!" She wiggled her snout once, twice, then — *aaa-chooo!* — her freezing sneeze sent a bridge of ice shooting across the flaming river.

"Yahoo!" cried Eric. "Julie, that's awesome. We can get through!"

"Hurry, before it melts!" said Keeah.

The little band of beasts raced over the frozen path and made it to the other side just as the bridge dissolved from the heat, and the fire leaped up once more.

Charging ahead, they soon came to the edge of a great wide forest, thick with trees and deep in shadow. It stretched as far as they could see in either direction.

"Another obstacle," said Sparr. "But it looks as if we can go right in. Let's just be on our guard."

"It's very dim here," said Max as they crept into the forest. "But not *too* bad —"

The deeper they went, the more the shadows surrounded them.

"I hear . . . scratching," said Keeah. "Does anyone else —"

Suddenly, a tree moved, thrusting a limb in front of the travelers. A branch behind them sprang alive. Long vines unwound from a third tree trunk and whipped wildly at the children.

"THE VEGETABLES ARE AFTER US!" Neal shouted.

Finally, one vine coiled around Max and tugged him off the ground.

"Oh, no, you don't!" cried Keeah. Lowering her antlers, she charged into the trees, crashing first one way, then the other, and freed Max. Julie sneezed icy breaths at the clutching branches, sending them shrieking and shriveling back to the treetops.

"Hurry out of here!" said Sparr, grabbing Julie and Max with his long, wolfen arms and pulling them away.

While the kids ran through the forest as quickly as they could, the air turned foggier and smokier until it was as thick and dark as night.

"Keep going," urged Keeah. "Forward —"

"No! Stop!" said Eric, his red eyes piercing the gloom. "I can see through this!"

Everyone stopped short. Moving slowly, Eric came to the edge of a deep chasm at the end of the forest. Looking down through heavy mist, he spied jagged rocks strewn across the bottom.

"I don't like having red eyes," he said, "but they helped me see the ravine. Without them, we would have fallen. Carefully, now. Follow me."

He led everyone along the edge of the ravine until they came to a narrow crossing.

"There's a desert on the far side," said

Eric, staring ahead. "Let's go. One at a time now . . ."

One by one, the six friends made their way over the ravine, then up a tall sand dune. When they got to the top, they stopped short. In front of them, and as far to the left and right as they could see, was a wall of sand swirling fifty feet high.

"The forge is probably beyond the sandstorm," said Sparr.

Blinking his rear eyes, Eric saw the plume of dust rising behind them over the black forest. "The beasts are coming closer every minute. Into the sandstorm, people."

As soon as they climbed down the dune — *whoosh!* — sand whipped up around them and biting winds tore at them.

"Hold together!" cried Keeah, one claw in Julie's short furry paw, the other clutching Max.

"Glup!" cried Julie. "Glup-glup-*glup*!"

"I CAN'T SEE ANYTHING!" Neal howled.

"I can't, either!" shouted Sparr. "But I guess I know what *my* beastie talent is. These ears were made for hearing. I hear . . . someone . . . munching crackers —"

"CRACKERS? IS THERE CHEESE, TOO?"

"No, but there's . . . an echo!" said Sparr, still cupping his ears. "An echo way out here means . . . we found a cave!"

Led by Sparr, the small band struggled forward until they found themselves at the mouth of a deep cave, half buried in the spinning sand.

As they stared into the darkness, a voice spoke from inside the cave.

"I say!" it said. "The weather is quite nasty out there. Do come in!"

Six

Welcome to My Cave

Even though the sandstorm was whirling and spinning around them, the children hesitated before the cave's entrance. They looked at one another, then back into the dark.

"Oh, don't be shy!" said the voice. "It's been ages since I've had visitors. Shake the sand from your paws and come in!"

Max turned to Keeah. "This is Bleak-wold," he whispered. "It could be a trick.

Who would want to invite beasts in, anyway?"

"Glu-up!" said Julie, nodding her furry blue head.

"But the voice told us to find the cave," said Eric.

"And that probably means to go in," whispered Keeah. "So let's go in. Carefully."

With a nod, Sparr folded back his ears and squeezed through the cave entrance.

Eric, Julie, and Keeah followed him in. Max and Neal brought up the rear.

The deeper into the cave passages they crept, the lighter it grew, until they came to a round, stony room beaming with light.

What they saw amazed them.

A large carpet hovered magically over the sandy floor. And just beneath it sat a thin man with a very long nose, a thick black mustache, a single eyebrow, and a tall floppy hat tipped with dozens of tiny bells.

Crisscrossing his chest was an array of colorful shawls and scarves. Several plump pouches and little bottles of liquid hung on a belt at his waist. And as the children stomped, slid, and staggered in, he adjusted a pair of green spectacles with lenses shaped like half-moons, blinked suddenly, jumped to his feet, and bowed.

"Princess Keeah!" he chirped. "Welcome!"

Keeah stared. "Wait. You can see the real us?"

"Yes, Princess!" he said. "These glasses show me that you're not really beasts."

"I hope the beasts don't have glasses like that," murmured Max.

"Oh, they couldn't," said the man with a little chuckle. "These are the only pair. I should know. I invented them. In fact, I invented everything you see here —"

Keeah gasped. "Oh, my gosh! You must be Pasha! The maker of my magic carpet! The maker of lots of magical things!"

"Guilty as charged!" the man said brightly. "Pasha *is* my name. Welcome to my little home away from home!"

Pasha's cave was filled with strange contraptions. The light beaming everywhere came from two small yellow blocks on the floor at his feet. Moving near them, Eric found that they shed warmth, too. Floating next to the hovering carpet was a slowly spinning globe. On it were moving images of Jaffa City, showing people everywhere, some even shopping in the market square. On the other side of the carpet was a little musical clock plinking away the seconds and minutes. Finally, leaning against the back wall was a staff of gnarled wood. On its tip was a life-size golden hand with its finger pointed straight out.

"Glup!" said Julie, her eyes wide in amazement.

"SHE MEANS — WOW!" shouted Neal.

"Ah, yes!" Pasha dug into two different pouches on his belt. "Here, a bracelet and a mint. Try them!"

Julie slipped the bracelet onto her wrist. "Glup you," she said. "Wait. I mean, thank you! I can talk again!"

Neal put the mint in his mouth. "Wow. I'm not shouting. I can talk in a regular voice. Awesome!"

Pasha bowed again. "And I love to hear you talk. I'm so glad you found me —"

Sparr's eyes widened. "Are you the mysterious voice who's been telling us to find the gate and find the cave? Giving us clues so that we'd find you?"

Pasha frowned, then shook his head.

"Sorry. I do a lot of things, but I don't do voices. In fact, I can't *do* magic myself. I simply *make* it. But what does that matter, when I can make this?"

Whoosh! From one of his pouches, he pulled an entire bowl of steaming noodles.

"Noodles," said Neal. "I love noodles —"

"Ah, but watch this," said Pasha. After he sprinkled a few grains of white dust into the soup as if he were seasoning it, the noodles began to unwind from the bowl, sticking straight up in the air and thickening until they formed long, stout ropes. "You can climb them. And nibble the noodles on the way up!"

Without thinking, Neal reached for the bowl. All at once — *splash!*

His three feet were suddenly wet. But when he looked down, the cave floor was perfectly dry.

"Invisible water," said Pasha. "I in-

vented it. I have no idea what it's good for yet. Here —"

He pulled a pinch of glittering orange dust from one of his many pouches and sprinkled it on the floor.

Sparr tapped his wolfen feet on the spot, and the floor was dry again.

"Awesome," said Julie. "I love how you make magic."

Pasha sighed. "Yes, well. Magic is what trapped me here, don't you know —"

"Oh!" said Keeah. She staggered once, then shut her eyes. "The voice . . . !"

Eric looked at her. "A new clue. What is he saying?"

Keeah's eyes opened. "He said . . . *find . . . the . . . ring* —"

Pasha jumped. "*I* was searching for a ring when I got trapped here!"

"Tell us all about it," said Sparr.

Pasha took a deep breath. "For ages, I'd

heard about a fabulous ring of the purest, whitest silver. In the old legends, it was known as the Ring of Midnight. Its power has something to do with the moon. Of course, I wanted to find the ring and study it."

Eric thought of the silver moon he had been seeing all day. "What does the Ring of Midnight do?"

"I never found out," Pasha told the children. "But it's not meant to be worn on a finger. No, no, it's about *this* big. . . . " He curved his thumb and middle finger into a half circle.

Neal nodded. "About the size of an English muffin pizza. Go on."

"When I'd heard that pirates had stolen the ring, along with lots of other magic, and hid it all here in this old pirate cave, I came to find it," said Pasha. "My magic helped get me this far —"

Eric gasped. "Pirate cave? Of course! This must be the hideout the fog pirates told us about. The beasts raided it and stole everything."

"Just so," said the magic maker. "The ring was already gone when I arrived. But whenever I tried to leave, the storm kept leading me right back here. I was trapped! I used the time well, though. I made things. Like this, for instance!"

He grabbed the strange wooden staff from the wall.

"I finished it this morning and was just going to try it when you arrived. Come, then. And cross your fingers — or claws!"

He ran through the passage to the cave entrance. Then, pressing a flat jewel mounted into the staff, he aimed its pointed finger out of the cave toward the sandstorm.

Suddenly, the winds parted in front of

the finger and a path opened through the swirling sand.

Pasha laughed. "It works! Now we can all go back to Doobesh together —"

"Wait!" said Sparr, touching his ears suddenly. "Out here, I can hear the beasts. They're already through the fire. They're getting closer."

Keeah turned to the little man. "Pasha," she said, "I'm sorry, but you'll have to go back to Doobesh without us. We really can't return until we destroy the magic forge."

Pasha wrinkled his eyebrow. "Did you say the . . . *magic* forge?"

Together the children told him why they were there, about Emperor Ko's forge, and how it used stolen magical objects to make armor for the beasts.

"A voice has been guiding us every inch of the way," said Eric. "First we had to find the dragon. When we found Jabbo, he said the voice had told him to find the gate. After going through the gate, Sparr helped us find the cave. Now the voice is telling us to find the ring —"

Keeah nodded at the little man. "Pasha, we have to go on. We have to find the ring. Then we have to destroy the forge."

"And then escape and live happily ever after," added Neal.

The magic maker listened to the children, pulling the ends of his mustache in deep thought. Finally, he said, "Five children and a spider troll out to save the world from a giant army of ferocious beasts? Sounds like all you need is a skinny little man to join you. Can I come?"

"Can you come?" said Keeah with a laugh. "Pasha, you're the best!"

"I'll settle for pretty good," Pasha said with a wink. "But some of my gadgets may be useful when we get to the forge. I must pack!" In a flash, he scampered back into the depths of the cave. Pulling down the carpet, he folded it to the size of a playing card and popped it into a pocket. He spun the globe to the size of a marble and collapsed the blocks of light until they were no larger than a pair of dice. In just moments, he took all the things in the cave, no matter how big, and bent, spun, and folded them into his pockets and pouches.

Then, leading the small group to the mouth of the cave, he lowered his staff. The finger pointed straight ahead, and a beam of golden light pressed into the storm, parting the sands before it.

Pasha grinned. "And now, as Neal would say, FOLLOW ME!"

Seven

At the Forge

The howl of the storm was deafening as Pasha led the group slowly forward. As quickly as the sand parted before the children, it swirled closed behind them.

"Because I'm not a wizard," said the magic maker, "my inventions work in the Dark Lands."

"Very handy in a sandstorm!" said Max, huddling close to Keeah.

Eric wondered how strange it might

look if anyone could see them. A many-scarfed little man with a long mustache leading six beasts through a sandstorm.

Suddenly, Sparr's ears twitched. He turned his head back. "I keep hearing the roar of the beasts. They're nearly through the forest now. We need to go faster."

"Keep going!" said Julie. "Keep going!"

They hurried through the storm for another twenty minutes or so, then finally stepped out of the whirlwind and onto a vast calm desert of gray sand.

"Oh, no," whispered Keeah, staring ahead.

"I'll say," said Neal. "Is that —?"

"I think so," said Eric. "Ko's magic forge."

Standing on the sands, surrounded by wisps of burnt grass and the stumps of broken, gnarled trees, was a giant black building. Its dark walls, reaching nearly to the gray clouds above it, glistened as if they were dripping with oil. Two huge smokestacks coiled up out of its insides, each one pouring out thick swirling smoke and spurts of blue and orange flames.

Thoom! Thoom! Even from far away, the kids could feel the ground thundering with what Eric guessed were giant hammers striking metal.

"The forge," repeated Sparr. "Where the beasts' magic armor is being made."

"And will be destroyed," said Julie.

"We have to make sure of that," said Keeah.

As they approached the giant forge, the smell of burning wood and the sharp odor of hot metal filled the air.

"There must be some beasts working there already," said Pasha, adjusting his glasses. "Luckily, they may not expect anyone but other beasts to have come this far. With your disguises, you can probably get us in. Then the fun starts."

Neal made a sound. "And by fun, you probably mean *not* fun?"

Pasha grinned. "I believe so, yes!"

Minutes later, they were standing before a giant open archway of iron. Peering in, they saw that the space inside the forge was nearly filled by a great black dome. It reached almost to the ceiling. From the top of the dome jutted pipes and tubes of all sizes. But over everything stood the enormous smokestacks, belching out flames and black smoke to the skies above.

Using the eyes in the back of his head, Eric could see the beasts entering the far side of the sandstorm. "We don't have a lot of time left," he said. "Maybe twenty minutes . . ."

"Then let's get moving," said Keeah.

Inside, they all ducked behind an anvil the size of a small car. Peering over and around it, they saw three very large beasts stomp out from behind the dome. They had huge red eyes and rough, leathery skin the color of dirt. Opening a hatch on the front of the dome, they dragged out a smoking piece of iron, set it on another anvil, and began pounding it with giant hammers.

Thooom! Thooom! With massive arms, the beasts battered the iron until it began to take the shape of a shield. They pounded out a center ridge as sharp as a blade, and curved spikes around the edges.

"Those beasts sure look fearsome," said Max.

"We're pretty fearsome, too, don't forget," said Julie.

"Except when you wiggle your snout like that," said Pasha with a giggle.

"I'm not wiggling my —" Julie raised a claw to her face. "Oh, no! My snout! Where is it going?"

Sparr's eyes widened. "Neal, your third foot. Keeah, your antlers —"

Max gasped. "The beast spell is ending! Oh, no!"

Eric's green fur shrank away and he was himself again. Sparr's body lost its wolflike shape, and his large ears dwindled into two regular ears and two small fins, while Max's four legs became eight once more.

In a matter of moments, the children and the spider troll were back to themselves.

"I can't believe it!" said Sparr. "The spell faded! It would take hours to do again. We don't have time. I'm sorry —"

"It's okay, Sparr," said Keeah. "You got us this far."

Pasha slipped off his green glasses and

folded them into a pocket. "Well, I, for one, am relieved. You were actually quite terrible to look at!"

"But now what do we do?" whispered Neal. "We're trapped in Ko's forge with three huge beasts, no magic, and lots more beasts on their way. How do we escape and live happily ever after?"

Eric watched the beasts heave the shield onto a pile of cooling armor and start on what looked like a helmet. "Guys, we might escape. But we won't live happily ever after — none of us will — unless we do what we planned to do. We need to find the ring and destroy this forge."

"But we're just ourselves now," said Julie.

Keeah looked at her, then at the beasts hammering faster and faster. She began to smile. "Just because we've lost our beast powers doesn't mean we can't outsmart them. If we work together the way we always have, we should be able to find the ring, destroy this place, *and* get out safely."

"That's the spirit!" said Pasha. "The stolen magical objects must be piled on the far side of the dome. If the Ring of Midnight hasn't been melted yet, you may find it there. Now, as for destroying —"

From a leather pouch on his belt, he pulled a little green box. Wires, tubes, and switches stuck out from its sides. "I call it my Blower-Upper. When it goes off, the whole forge will go *kaboom*!"

Keeah smiled. "I like that sound. Sparr, Pasha, Eric, Max — you're in charge of *kaboom*. Julie, Neal, come with me! We don't have much time to find that ring. Let's move!"

Keeping to the shadows, Keeah, Neal, and Julie darted away to the far side of the dome.

Thoom-thoom-thoom! The beasts were now busy hammering a double-pointed spear into shape.

Pasha unwound two small pouches from his belt and gave one each to Sparr and Eric. "When I say so, toss these into the furnace. They'll make a bit of a flash, which will distract the beasts and cool the flames enough for me to get to the dome. Max, here —"

He slipped a small red disk from a pocket, tapped it, and gave it to the spider troll.

Max looked at it, then blinked. "A clock!"

"When I set the Blower-Upper," said Pasha, "start the clock running at thirty minutes. We'll need to know how much time we have before the *kaboom*."

"Galen would be proud of us!" said Max, holding the clock firmly. "And of me!"

"Now, before I set this," said Pasha, "how many pieces do we want the forge to blow up into? A hundred or a thousand?"

Eric turned to Sparr. They both grinned.

"A million!" they chimed.

Pasha smiled, too. "Great minds work alike. Now the distraction. Go, boys!"

Eric and Sparr carefully worked their way along the walls until they were near the furnace opening. A moment later, Pasha gave the signal.

The boys tossed the pouches into the furnace.

Tzzzzz! Fssssshh! Whoooom!

A fountain of sparks sprayed out of the furnace ten, fifteen feet in the air.

"Arrrghh!" The beasts at the anvil howled. They staggered back from the fire.

Without being seen, Pasha dashed to the dome and set the Blower-Upper. When he raced back, Max started the clock ticking. "Thirty minutes!"

Eric waved across the dome at Keeah, but the princess didn't move.

"Something's wrong," said Sparr. "Let's get over there —"

Making their way carefully to the far side of the dome, they found Keeah, Julie, and Neal hunched behind a third anvil, even larger than the first two.

"This place will go *kaboom* in minutes," said Eric. "Did you find the ring? What's the matter?"

"We found all the magical objects," said the princess. "Look."

Not far away was another, much larger opening into the furnace. Just outside it was a mound of crumpled metal goblets, gold chests, crowns, bracelets, wands, jewels, and other magical objects. Next to it were three more red-eyed, dirt-colored beasts. Every few seconds, they shoveled more objects into the furnace.

And there, sitting on top of the pile of magical things, was a large silver ring. In the light of the fire, it gleamed brighter than anything else in the heap.

Eric knew instantly that it was unlike the other objects. His heart began to pound as if he were in the presence of some of the most powerful magic he had ever known.

"Oh, my goodness!" gasped Pasha. "It's the Ring of Midnight!"

The very next instant, one of the beasts dug his shovel into the pile.

Then, with a quick heave, he hurled the ring into the fire.

Eight

Ride the . . . What?

"Oh, no!" whispered Neal. "I can't believe it! After all this!"

The small group stared into the furnace, watching the silver ring glisten in the flame far more brightly than anything around it.

As the beasts shoveled more objects into the fire, Pasha's eyes gleamed in the firelight. "Oh, dear, dear. The legends were true. It is a ring of fabulous beauty. I know magic, and I can tell you, that harbors some great power."

"All the more reason we can't let it be melted into Ko's armor!" whispered Keeah.

"But how do we get it?" asked Julie.

"With only . . . twenty-four minutes left!" added Max.

Eric turned to Pasha. "The dust we threw into the furnace. You said it cooled the flames. For how long?"

Sparr blinked. "Eric, are you saying . . . wait, what *are* you saying?"

Eric stared at the fire, then up at the smokestacks. "I don't know what I'm saying, except that the voice called us to find the ring, and we can't leave here without it! —"

"Rrrr-grrr!" There came a sudden sound of roaring and grunting outside the forge. A second later, the giant arched doorway was filled with grumbling beasts. The dirt-colored forge workers stomped over to them.

"I didn't think things could get much more dangerous," said Julie. "But they just did. How can we get that ring back —"

. "In twenty-one minutes!" whispered Max, holding up the little clock.

Neal grinned suddenly. "Noodles! Pasha's *magical* noodles. What if we ride them all the way up to the top of the smokestacks and down inside? If the fire is still cool, we can get the ring and get back out again, and the beasts will never know!"

"Ride . . . the noodles?" said Pasha. "I say, Neal, what a brilliant idea. I'll stay here, and you help one another into the smokestack!"

Careful to keep hidden from the beasts, Pasha quickly pulled a steaming bowl of soup out of a pouch, set it on the floor, and seasoned it. In seconds, noodles began to grow and twist up from it. While Pasha stayed below, the kids and Max clung to the noodles as they rose like magical ropes up the shadowy inside wall of the forge.

More and more beasts entered the forge. Their roaring and cawing and chattering became louder and louder.

Reaching the top of one smokestack, Eric swung his noodle back and forth until he was able to swing it into the top of the smokestack. Neal, Julie, Keeah, and Sparr followed right behind. Still clutching tight, they rode the noodles down into the furnace.

"Good thing Pasha cooled the fire," said Neal. "I don't want to be roasted!"

Finally, the six friends dropped to the floor of the furnace amid piles of flaming coals, half-heated armor, and shining magical objects. The fire was cool, but it was rapidly getting hotter.

"I see the ring!" murmured Sparr. Leaping into the cool flames, he grabbed the ring from the coals. As he did, his eyes went wide. His face twisted in an expression of pain. "Ahhh!"

"What is it?" asked Keeah, hurrying to him. "Is the ring hot?"

"No!" Sparr staggered to his knees. "But . . . take it!"

Keeah took it from him, then blinked. "What's wrong? I don't feel anything —"

"Talk later," said Max. "Sixteen minutes!"

Eric helped Sparr up. He still didn't know the truth about the Ring of Midnight. No one knew whose voice had urged them to find the ring. No one understood what powers it possessed.

Could the ring's magic be something special only to Sparr? Eric looked at the boy. Sparr was staring at Keeah as she

looped the silver ring onto her belt, the fins behind his ears as red as the coals themselves.

What was *the Ring of Midnight, after all*? he wondered.

But now the flames were building higher. Heat rose from the pile of coals and metal.

"Getting hot!" said Julie tugging the noodles. "Pasha! Back up!"

Almost at once, the noodles began to draw them back up the smokestack. Very soon they heard the sounds of little explosions, popping and crackling, and the sounds of yelling.

"Uh-oh," said Neal. "I think the beasts know we're here!"

"Hurry! Keep going!" urged Max.

When they were outside the smokestack again, they saw Pasha tossing fireworks, trying to keep the beasts away from the noodles. By the time the kids were down on the forge floor, the beasts were massing together, growling and shaking their claws and fists.

Pasha ran to the children. "The beasts aren't too happy with us, I'm afraid!"

"We got the ring," said Keeah. "Let's get out of here now —"

"Sooner than now!" chirped Max. "We have only . . . eleven minutes!"

"This should give us the time we need to escape," Pasha said.

He tossed a tiny, pea-sized object at the beasts. It whistled loudly, then — *poomf!* — a shower of sparks exploded, throwing the beasts back to the walls.

"Okay, Pasha, unfold your famous magic carpet," said Eric. "We need to fly!"

"Fly?" said Pasha with a weak smile. "Ah, yes. About that. Well, you see, that is to say, I mean . . . I never fly!"

Nine

The Great Race

"Groooo!" The beasts began staggering up from the floor.

"Whaaaat!" cried Keeah, backing up to the forge wall. "But you're Pasha! Of Pasha's flying carpets!"

The magic maker nodded. "Some with very nice designs on them! But it's the *flying* part of the flying carpet I don't care for. I'm rather afraid of heights, you see —"

Some of the beasts were now pulling weapons from the pile of forged armor.

"But you just set a bomb in the beastie forge in the Bleakwold section of the Dark Lands!" said Julie. "Pasha, you're fearless!"

He shrugged. "Apparently not so much."

Quivering, Max held up the clock. "Excuse me, but we only have ten and a half minutes. We must turn the bomb off, or we'll all go *kaboom!*"

"Can't," said Pasha. "The Blower-Upper doesn't turn off. So the beasts can't stop it, you know."

The armed beasts formed a line and began to stomp closer to the children.

"It looks like they want to stop *us,*" said Neal.

Pasha tossed another pea-sized ball. *Pooomf!* The beasts were pushed back, but this time, their shields protected them. They kept coming.

"We'll never get out of here in time," said Julie, backing up until she hit the wall. "Pasha, don't you have anything that can help?"

The man frowned. "Nothing I can think of. Well, except this." He opened a pouch and tugged out what looked like a miniature comb.

Neal stared at it. "Uh-huh. So when the beasts get us, we can look our best?"

Pasha chuckled. "Oh, dear, no. It gets bigger."

As the beasts stomped closer, Pasha tugged one end of the comb. A little wheel came out. He spun it, and it became as large as a small bicycle wheel. Pulling on the other end, Pasha made a set of handlebars and another wheel emerge. With his long fingers stretching and flipping and turning with amazing speed, a seat appeared, then five more seats, then a sidecar,

then a small sail, a pair of skis, two propellers, and a balloon.

By the time he was done, the thing sitting on the ground in front of them looked
like a flying, skiing, rolling bicycle.

With a motor.

"I call it the Pashamobile," he said.

"I call it our way out of here," Eric said
with a laugh. "All aboard. Now!"

Putt-putt-vroooom! The little machine
blew out a cloud of steam and shot away
from the furnace. It drove straight into the
beasts.

"Groooo!" cried the beasts, dodging left
and right. "Arrrrgh!"

Those that didn't scatter out of the way
were knocked back into one another as the
Pashamobile burst through them. It raced
away from the dome, swerved to the door,
and roared out onto the plains.

"Yes! We made it!" cried Julie.

"Doobesh, here we come!" yelled Keeah.

It took just moments for the kids to master the controls. Max pedaled furiously from his seat, his eight legs a blur of speed. Neal spun a set of giant gears that ran the large propeller, while Julie powered the smaller one with a set of twisted levers. Eric steered with the handlebars next to them, while Sparr raised and lowered the skis and Keeah worked a set of small sails on the rear.

And as they roared across the countryside, Pasha sat cross-legged in his cushy sidecar, pointing. "That way. Around that tree. Over those rocks. Faster, please. We have —"

"Only seven minutes!" cried the spider troll.

"Roooaaarrrrr!" The beasts charged angrily from the forge.

Mounting Pasha's staff on the front of the machine, the children plowed through the sandstorm and shot toward the ravine. They were going so fast, they drove straight across the ravine and were on the far side before the vehicle had a chance to fall.

"Wait! Slow down," said Pasha. "I have an idea!"

Neal and Eric together slowed the vehicle. Pasha sprinkled a light blue dust across the ground behind them. Then he tapped the dust with the tip of his staff.

Splash . . .

"Excellent," he said. "Invisible water. Now go!"

Vrrrm! They took off into the foggy forest. As they raced between the trees, they heard splashing, then roaring, and finally the sound of slurping.

"They crossed the ravine, but stopped to drink!" said Eric. "They won't catch us!"

"We'll see," said Max. "Five and a half minutes to go."

When they came to the fiery river, the flames were leaping as high as ever.

"Makes you wish I still had icy beast breath, doesn't it?" said Julie.

"This is better!" said Pasha. He touched a button in the sidecar and all of a sudden two large springs jerked down from the front of the Pashamobile like a giant pair of legs. They slammed the ground and — *boing!* — the vehicle bounced up and over the flaming river. *Wump! Wump!* They thudded down on the far side, bounced high, then landed right onto the lowered land skis and took off again.

Mile after mile, they tore across the plains, racing over the charred earth until they finally blasted through the Bleakwold

gate, and spotted the twisting towers of Doobesh in the far distance.

"Ah, Doobesh," sang Pasha. "How long has it been since I've seen you? Oh, your towers. Your blue walls. Your — watch for that ditch!"

"Don't slow down!" cried Max. "Four minutes and counting!"

Eric puffed and puffed. "Keep going!"

Sparr worked the skis over every bump. Neal and Julie spun their propellers wildly. Doobesh loomed closer.

"Oh, man . . . oh, man!" cried Sparr. "Faster . . . *faster* —"

"Forty seconds," said Max.

The beasts thundered across the countryside behind them, getting closer by the second. The Pashamobile practically flew into Doobesh, covering the last few yards and blasting through the giant blue gate when all of a sudden —

Wham!

They crashed into something hard, tumbled out of the Pashamobile, and spilled to the ground in a heap.

The something hard they crashed into was a pair of knees.

Only they weren't the puffy brown knees of Jabbo the pie maker.

They were the black, stone-hard knees of a moon dragon.

"Gethwing!" gasped Sparr, scrambling away from him.

Gethwing raised himself up as high as he could go. His four wings, ragged and spiked, arched up behind him. His large domed head with its massive drooling jaw turned down to the children. His eyes burned like two fiery coals. Flames sizzled between his long, curved fangs. Lifting his mighty clawed hands over the children, he prepared to strike.

All of a sudden, Max jumped up and held Pasha's clock high. "Excuse me, Mr. Gethwing — just a moment. Five, four, three . . ."

Two seconds later, they saw it, heard it, and felt it.

KAAAA —

Ten

A Lot to Do

—*BOOOOOOOM!*

The whole dark sky erupted in a blaze of yellow flame.

Far away, giant chunks of iron flew straight up, then slammed back to earth with the sound of thunder. The blast rolled across Bleakwold, across the lands between, and shook the towers and walls of Doobesh itself.

The force knocked Gethwing flat on his

back, while the kids were thrown into a tangle of arms and legs.

"Yahoo!" yelped Neal. "That forge is history! Blown to a thousand little bits!"

"A million!" cried Pasha, bouncing with glee. "My Blower-Upper really works!"

In the far distance, an enormous plume of orange flames and black smoke poured up to the sky.

Gethwing staggered to his feet and roared, fire bursting from his mouth. At the same time, the beasts from the forge crawled into the city, hissing and steaming from the blast. They gathered around Gethwing, staring at the children.

In that moment, time seemed to stop.

"Do you think Gethwing's mad?" asked Keeah, huddling with her friends near the wreckage of the Pashamobile. "I think he's mad —"

"Kallo-tem-na-toof! Nembo-sama-fah!" shrieked Gethwing.

As one, the dark beasts raised their claws. They took a step toward the children.

Suddenly, a cry came down from the rooftops. "Doobesh for the Doobeshians!"

Before anyone could make a move, a thick black net dropped over the children, Max, and Pasha, and — *fwing!* — swept them up to a rooftop filled with furry little Doobeshians and big burly pirates. And in the middle of the pirates stood a small dragon wearing a chef's hat.

"Jabbo!" cried Keeah.

"And friends!" said the little dragon. "Everyone — *now!*"

At Jabbo's cry, the rooftops across the city suddenly came alive with pirates and Doobeshians hurling bricks down on the beasts.

Gethwing and the others shrieked and bellowed. They flew up at their attackers, but the pirates dropped more nets on them, and the Doobeshians hurled brick after brick in their direction. Every new advance of the beasts was met with squirts of hot pie filling, and they fell back to the gates of the city again and again.

"Jabbo, are we glad to see you!" said Eric, tossing bricks one after another.

"And Jabbo to see you!" said the pie maker. "No sooner had you and the beasts entered Bleakwold than the real Gethwing came. Luckily, the Doobeshians and the pirates hid poor Jabbo. Until now! More bricks here! More pie filling there! Attack!"

With loud calls from both Jabbo and Yoho, the pirates and Doobeshians leaped down from the roofs and raced through alleys, flashing their swords and sticks, whooping and cheering.

The beasts charged back, but the fog pirates — as good as their name — vanished in a cloud of fog. The beasts, with Gethwing at their head, tried to battle the fog, but more bricks and more pie filling rained down on them, and invisible sticks whacked at them.

Shielding himself, Gethwing gave out a long shriek. *"Path-na-ta-Ko!"*

The beasts gathered around him. A moment later, Gethwing led the beast army crashing out through the blue gates and back toward the Dark Lands. Into the smoky air they went, drawing the dark skies with them as they retreated.

Sparr whooped. "Yes! They're going! All the way back to Ko!"

With the smoke and clouds gone, the sun blazed once again on Doobesh's streets.

The battle was over.

"Yahoo, Yoho!" cried the pirates, turning visible again. They shook their fists and waved their swords in the air, crying, "Doobesh is free!"

"Yes, free!" echoed the Doobeshians.

"We did it," said Eric. "I can't believe it. The beasts are gone."

"Good riddance," snarled Jabbo, adjusting his chef's hat.

"The beasts *are* gone," said Yoho, moving his eye patch from one eye to the other. "But if they come back, I think we'll be ready for them. That is, if . . ."

The pirate captain now turned to Jabbo and slapped the dragon's shoulder. "We'll be ready for them if . . . you, Jabbo, will be our leader in Doobesh? After all, we like your pies!"

"Pies!" shouted the Doobeshians.

The little dragon smiled from ear to ear, even as he blushed. "Jabbo? Your leader?"

"Jabbo, our king!" cheered the Doobeshians.

The pie maker drew in a deep breath. "Jabbo accepts!" he said. "If Princess Keeah approves, that is."

Keeah adjusted her crown, straightened her tunic, and smiled at the little dragon. "Jabbo, you helped us today like a true friend. You are officially free. Now, if you and the pirates can agree to stop stealing magic . . ."

"Stop stealing!" said Yoho. He frowned. Then he grumbled. Finally, he nodded. "Mostly," he said.

Keeah looked sternly at the pirate captain, then smiled. "We'll work on that. In the meantime, Jabbo, I pronounce you King of Doobesh. Bake pies. Be a just and fair ruler. And try to be good!"

"King Jabbo!" cried the furry Doobeshians.

As Yoho and his mates broke into song, the pirates hoisted Jabbo on their shoulders and carried the new king through the cheering crowds.

Soon, the children, Max, and Pasha were standing alone in the sunny streets in front of the palace.

"Ah! I like to see things end so happily," said Pasha.

"We owe much of it to you," said Max, shaking the little man's hand.

"And I to you," returned the magic maker. "Princess, Max, may I join you in Jaffa City? It is, after all, the most magical place of all. And perfect for a magic maker."

Keeah smiled. "That would be wonderful."

"Let's go there now," said Sparr. "I think our work in Doobesh is done!"

In a swirl of spinning blue light, the

seven friends left the strange, sun-filled city of Doobesh and whirled through the air to Jaffa City.

By the time they were all back in Galen's tower, night was beginning to fall. Through the tower window Eric could see the moon as he remembered it in his world, sitting just above the horizon like a silver globe.

Julie smiled suddenly. "Every adventure is a journey and every journey is an adventure. This was sure both."

"It took just two days," said Eric. "But it seems like a lifetime."

"Galen would love hearing about our adventure," said Max. "We destroyed the forge. We found the magic ring. He would be quite proud of us."

Keeah unlooped the ring from her belt and held it up. "The voice told us step by step how to find the ring," she said. "But we still don't know who wanted us to find it."

"Or why," said Sparr. "When I touched it, I felt . . ." He looked as if he were searching for a word. Finally, he shook his head. "It has some kind of power, that's all I know."

Eric wondered about that. What kind of power did the ring have exactly? And whose voice kept pushing them to find it?

"Can I see it?" asked Neal. Taking it from Keeah, he slipped it on his wrist.

"Not your style," said Julie.

"You don't think it's for a giant, do you?" asked Pasha as Neal gave it to Eric.

Still looking at Sparr, Eric took the ring. The moment he did, his heart thudded in his chest. The ring felt burning hot, then as cold as ice. It felt as if it weighed a ton. His legs gave out beneath him and he staggered to the floor under its weight.

"Eric!" said Keeah, rushing to him.

Struggling to hold it up to her, he gasped suddenly. "No — wait!"

In the center of the silver ring, framed by the silver circle, he saw the moon.

But an instant later, it wasn't the moon he saw in the center of the ring.

It was the face of a man.

"I see him!" said Eric.

Everyone bent down to look. They saw it, too.

"Oh!" said Max. "It's . . . it's . . . Galen!"

It was Galen's face.

But, amazingly, he was not the old white-haired man they had last seen. His beard was darker and shorter, his face rosier, his eyes sparkling. Galen was younger.

He was wearing a green turban studded with bright red rubies.

And he was smiling.

"Galen!" gasped Max. "You are well. Better than well. You look younger!"

When Galen spoke, they all heard his voice, no longer in a whisper, but clear and strong and loud.

. *I am proud of you!* Galen said. *Your journey was a long one, and difficult. But you found the dragon, the gate, the cave, and the ring. There remains but one thing more. Using the ring, you must now . . . find me!*

A moment later, the wizard's face, still smiling, faded, and the ring was a ring once more.

Keeah whooped. "Yes! Galen's coming back!" She took the ring from Eric and set it in a bowl on a table.

Still weak from holding the ring, Eric breathed deeply. He knew Sparr was looking at him. Their eyes met. What the power of the Ring of Midnight was—and why it affected only them—was a story for another day.

All of a sudden, the round room lit up with a rainbow-colored light. The magic stairs hovered outside the tower window.

"Time to go," said Julie.

"But we'll be back soon," said Neal.

"To help us find Galen," added Max.

"And help us stop Ko once and for all," said Sparr.

Eric nodded. "Yeah. We have a lot to do."

"A *lot* to do," Keeah repeated with a smile.

The three friends climbed out the window and onto the stairs. The last thing Eric saw as they entered the pink clouds was the large silver moon.

It was shining more brightly than ever.

"I'm glad we're not beasts anymore," said Neal as they reached the upper stairs.

"My mom always says I grow out of my sneakers too fast. Just think if I had three feet!"

Julie laughed and checked her watch. "Speaking of moms, my mom's waiting for us. We're just in time for supper."

They rushed into the closet at the top of the stairs. The moment they turned on the light, the staircase vanished, and —

Dingdong! The front doorbell rang.

Eric froze. "Holy cow! I bet there really *was* someone watching us at the movies! And they followed us here. . . ."

Slipping carefully from the closet, the three friends turned off the light, closed the door, and pushed the two cartons in front of it. Quietly, they made their way upstairs to the front door.

"My heart is pounding like those beastie hammers," said Julie.

"Everybody just try to be cool," said Eric.

"I'll try . . . to try," whispered Neal.

Eric went to the front door. Slowly, he opened it.

He blinked. Standing there was a girl just about their age. She was tall and had long, black hair. Her eyes were the darkest Eric had ever seen.

"Hi," she said. "I just moved into the house at the end of the street. I'm Meredith."

"Uh . . . hi," said Eric, trying to sound calm.

The girl tucked some loose strands of hair behind one ear and held out her hand. "I just wanted to say that you dropped these on the street. You were all running kind of crazy."

In her hand were Neal's sunglasses.

"Wow, thanks," he said, taking them. "I really thought I lost them."

"No problem," she said. "I also wanted to say thanks for the cookies you left at my house the other day. That was nice. Well, see you later. I know you have a lot to do."

The three friends watched the girl walk back up the street and go into the big house at the corner.

"A lot to do?" said Eric. "That's what we said in Droon. . . ."

"I remember," said Julie. "But she seems okay. Not a beast or anything. Just normal. What did she say her name was? Meredith?"

Eric nodded slowly. "Still, Droon has to stay a secret. We have to be prepared for anything. We have to be really careful."

"Even sneaky," said Neal, sliding on his dark glasses. "I know I'm ready."

The Adventure Continues in
The Secrets of Droon #25
The Riddle of Zorfendorf Castle

It was noon on a warm Saturday when Eric Hinkle sat down on a sunny beach with his friends, Neal and Julie.

He looked around and smiled. "Guys, this is the life."

"I know," agreed Neal. "This beach has all my favorite stuff. Sun and fun and . . . what's the third thing? Oh, yeah. Cheeseburgers, hot dogs, onion rings, curly fries, and vanilla shakes —"

Eric laughed. "That's like . . . six things!"

"Not the way Neal eats," said Julie. "He's the original human blender!"

Neal looked thoughtful for a moment. "Blender Boy. I like it!"

The beach near Eric's house was a narrow strip of sand at the edge of a small pond. On one side was a tiny concession stand. On the other was a parking lot.

In between were kids and parents from his neighborhood, sunning and playing and having fun.

"The water is so beautiful," said Julie, gazing out at the far side of the pond where their gym teacher, Mr. Frando, was tossing a large net into the water. "It's kind of like the color of sapphires."

"It's kind of like the Sea of Droon," Neal whispered. "Only in our world."

Eric smiled again.

Droon was the mysterious and magical world he and his friends had discovered under his house one day. Droon was where they had met Princess Keeah, a powerful young wizard. It was where they helped her battle an evil sorcerer known as Lord Sparr.

And it was where Eric and Julie had gotten magical powers. Julie had gained the ability to fly and sometimes to change shape, while Eric was fast becoming an actual wizard.

Each time the friends descended the rainbow-colored staircase in his basement — and they had gone down those steps many times — things in Droon had gotten more fabulous, more exciting, and more dangerous.

Julie sighed. "Keeah would love this. Too bad she probably doesn't have much time to just hang out. Especially now that things are a little weird — "

"A lot weird," said Neal, looking at the concession stand and starting to frown.

Eric felt the same way.

Things in Droon really had gotten strange.

First of all, Sparr had recently woken a four-armed, three-eyed, bull-headed beast named Ko from a four-century nap. Now, Ko ruled over a dark army of fearsome beasts.

Stranger still, in waking up Ko, Sparr himself had been transformed into a boy. He was now on their side, helping them stop Ko from turning Droon into his smelly Dark Lands. . . .

Eric expected to be called back to Droon at any minute to start the search. "I packed the magic soccer ball in case Keeah sends for us."

"At least some things haven't changed," said Julie. "The ball still calls us to Droon. And the staircase still takes us. I can't wait to go — "

"Maybe I'll get in line now," said Neal.

"Get in line? For the staircase?" asked Eric.

Neal shook his head. "For lunch. The concession stand is getting really busy."

He bounced up from the blanket, then he pointed across the pond. "But call me if Mr. Frando catches any fish sticks out there!"

For the next few minutes, Eric and Julie watched as Neal worked his way inch by inch to the head of the food line.

He was nearly at the counter when Eric caught sight of a tall girl standing on the beach behind them. She had long, wavy hair and the darkest eyes he had ever seen.

Julie saw her, too and made a low growling noise. "Meredith! She's everywhere."

Eric had to admit it. The girl *was* everywhere. She had just moved into a house on his street. She went to their school. She had even come to his house.

The girl had only been around for a

few days, and already Eric was certain she had heard them talking about Droon.

"Whenever I even *think* about Droon, she's there," said Julie. "We have to be careful."

Eric kept his eyes fixed on the girl. "Right," he whispered. "Careful. Because Droon has to stay a secret —"

Suddenly, Julie grabbed his arm. "Oh, my gosh, Eric, look —"

He turned to see Neal, his arms filled with trays and boxes and giant cups, heading straight for a deep hole some children had dug in the sand.

Eric nearly choked. "Oh, no! Neal!"

Neal peered over his food. "Coming —"

"He'll fall in!" said Julie.

Without thinking, Eric flicked the index finger of his right hand.

Zzzzzt! A single silver spark flew across the sand, whizzing past coolers and around beach chairs. Just as Neal lowered his foot toward the hole — *pooomf!* — a small explosion of sand filled the hole.

Neal stepped firmly on it and kept walking.

Eric grinned. "Ha! That was awesome!"

"Not so awesome!" said Julie. "That nosy girl saw you! Meredith saw you! She's coming right here!"

About the Author

Tony Abbott is the author of more than fifty funny novels for young readers, including the popular *Danger Guys* books and *The Weird Zone* series. Since childhood he has been drawn to stories that challenge the imagination, and, like Eric, Julie, and Neal, he often dreamed of finding doors that open to other worlds. Now that he is older — though not quite as old as Galen Longbeard — he believes he may have found some of those doors. They are called books. Tony Abbott was born in Ohio and now lives with his wife and two daughters in Connecticut.

For more information about Tony Abbott and the continuing saga of Droon, visit www.tonyabbottbooks.com.